A PUG BOAT FAMILY

FULL STEAM AHEAD

WRITTEN & ILLUSTRATED BY LAURA BERGSMA

Down by the bay, near a little harbor,
lived a little pug with his father and grandfather.
They were known by the last name Pugsley, the first name Charles.
The Pugsley family was small — they wore small hats and small coats,
they even ran a business driving small Pug Boats.

Charles the 1st — we'll call him Grandfather,
was the first Pugsley to work down at the harbor.
Way back in the day, before his beard was gray,
he'd launch his little boat into the water
to pull in barges of bones for filling the town's larders.

In exchange for the tow Grandpa Puglsey provided
he could take as many bones home as he decided.
Yet, this is how he provided for his young son Charles —
He gathered just enough for the day's needs
and he never felt needy, he never felt poor, and he never felt greedy.

But one day as he watched
his young son play,
Grandfather's mind got
carried away...

It whispered a small fear right into his small floppy ear.
It spoke very quietly, but it spoke very clearly —
"What if you can't provide for the son that you love so dearly?
What if there is a storm and the boats don't arrive?
If you take *only* for the days needs, *how will you both survive?*"

Now, Grandfather Pugsley was born with a smooth face —
but with this thought, an interesting thing took place.
As he dwelt upon the *how*, wrinkles began to form
on his previously smooth brow.
And with each new wrinkle, Grandfather hatched a plan,
of how he and young Charles would always have enough bones on hand...

Every night he would tote home
a few extra bones in the pockets of his coat!
He filled up his cupboards and he filled up his larder,
but Grandfather decided he still must work harder.
What if the barges are gone not one day, but two?
Or three or four? Then what would he do?
So he carried home sacks, and inside their home he built up stacks,
and when he ran out of room, he began to bury the bones out back...

All the while, young Charles was watching.
He was watching the hurry.
He was watching the panic.
He was watching the worry.

Charles I

Now working so hard
made Grandfather quite gruff.
So he sat young Charles down and said
"Son, this life is ruff,
you can never know
if there will be enough."

So Grandfather's lesson was heeded,
and Charles worked alongside him
to bring home more bones
than needed.

And he grew up
to be just like Grandfather,
always worried,
always striving harder.

Then one day Charles the 2nd — we can now call him "Father"
was watching *his* young son play, and his mind too got carried away...
It whispered a new fear into *his* small floppy ear.
It spoke very quietly, but it spoke very clearly —
"What if you can't provide for the son you love so dearly?"
"You have saved a lot, *but* what if your bones begin to mold?"
"What if they begin to rot?"
Father's wrinkles deepened with this new thought,
and as *his* wrinkles grew, Father came up with *his* own plot...

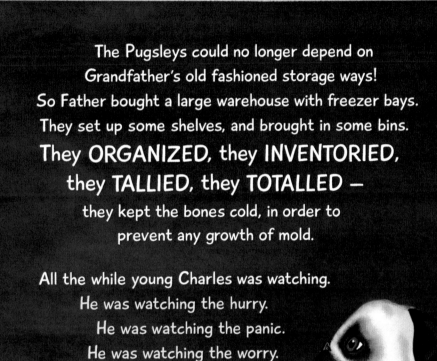

The Pugsleys could no longer depend on
Grandfather's old fashioned storage ways!
So Father bought a large warehouse with freezer bays.
They set up some shelves, and brought in some bins.
They **ORGANIZED**, they **INVENTORIED**,
they **TALLIED**, they **TOTALLED** —
they kept the bones cold, in order to
prevent any growth of mold.

All the while young Charles was watching.
He was watching the hurry.
He was watching the panic.
He was watching the worry.

And as Grandfather had
done so long ago,
Father sat down *his* own son,
so that he would be in the know.
"Son", he said,
"this life is ruff,
and you can never be
prepared enough."

Charles I

April
15

So he learned about accounting and he learned about the files,
then Father put him to work organizing the paper piles.
And Charles grew up to be just like Father,
always worried, always striving harder.

As the three generations of Pugsleys worked,
they pondered, and this caused their
list of fears to grow longer.
Their list of fears grew downright silly —
could these things happen, Really?!?

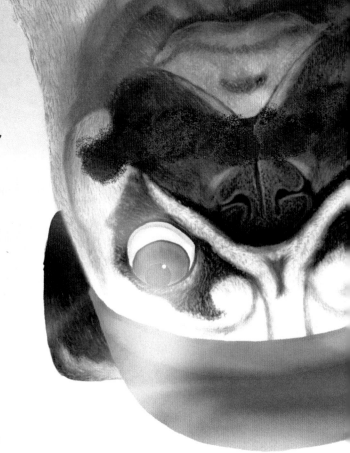

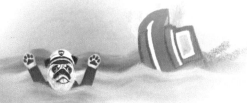

What if those bones are too heavy a load?
What if that makes my
Pug Boat explode?

What if an elephant
breaks into our warehouse?
What if the bones get
eaten by a mouse?

What if I get infested
with ticks and fleas?
What if I get stung by
ferocious honey bees?

Their thoughts spun round and round
and with each rising doubt,
their wrinkles squeezed so tight
they felt their eyes might POP OUT!

Then one day Charles the 3rd — we'll just call him "Charles",
was watching Father and Grandfather toil away
when *his* thoughts began to play...

"You certainly have collected the most,
but does your collection include a fine roast?
If you had some steaks to smell,
then you would *really* be getting along well."
Suddenly, Charles's eyes grew large,
as he spotted something shiny
on the deck of the barge.

Perhaps, owning the most was an idea outdated,
but owning the best just might give his family some rest.
A chest that looked like a treasure,
surely must contain meat beyond measure!

However, the chest was closed
and appeared to be locked,
so Father and Grandfather refused
to bring it down to the dock.

What was in it, they just could not see —
It could contain bats or ticks or fleas!
It might contain nothing,
and that was a risk,
a risk that neither elder Puglsey
was willing to pick.

So Charles the 3rd came up with *his* own plans
of how he could get that crate into his own hands.
With his *own* license through hard work and learning,
he could drive his *own* boat and choose his *own* earning.
So he studied the harbor rule book late at night,
he studied 'til the wee hours by candlelight.

Day after day, he focused on this task.
He was feeling quite smart,
he was feeling quite wise,
but one night a *new fear* struck him
right between the eyes.

It whispered very quietly,
but it whispered quite clearly
"What if you never obtain
that chest you hold so dearly?

What if you *don't pass* your
Pug Boat license test?
What if you and your family
never find rest?"

The night before the big test,
Charles tossed and turned.
He was anxious and his stomach churned...

However, when he passed his test
the next morning, it was no surprise —
since Charles was so prepared and so wise.
Today was the day he'd ensure the Pugsleys were *well* fed.
With his license in hand, into the harbor his little boat tread.

Ahead was his prize — when he got there
he knew exactly what he would do.
He would tow in that barge, and for his payment
he'd choose the crate that was shiny and large.

But, beyond the barge loomed a dark cloud...
The wind began to blow, his boat began to rock.
Charles's fears rose up and his face wrinkled in thought —
"This life *is* ruff, and now I see that there will never
be enough... Not enough planning, not enough time,
not enough hard work can fetch
what should be mine!"

With this thought, a giant wave CRASHED!
Charles watched horrified,
as into the water all the crates splashed.

Desperately, he leapt to retrieve his treasure.
Clinging on, he tried to keep it afloat,
but no matter his effort,
he was sinking fast under the boats.

Father and Grandfather raced to the scene.
"Charles!" They screamed,
"You are not without hope,

LET GO! LET GO!

and we'll throw you a rope!"

But Charles was stubborn.
He held onto his way.
All the way down
to the bottom
of the bay.

There he sat and became more concerned,
"What if the meat on these bones *has* turned?"

And while his mind started to race,
the "*What Ifs*" started to increase in pace.

"What if this crate *is* full of ticks or fleas?"
"Or just contains ferocious honey bees?"
"What if Grandfather never tastes a fine roast?"
"What if Father has no reason to boast?"
"What if my family never has the best?"

And with his last breath came the
last "*What If?*" Charles could express —

"What if we never ever find rest?"

When that "What If?" reached the surface,

IT POPPED!

And Charles Pugsley let go.

He let go of his grip, he let go of his hurry,
he let go of his panic, he let go of his worry.
His face began to unwrinkle.
His brow began to unfurrow.
His body began to rise.

As his weight lifted off the crate
a funny thing happened...
The lid opened up and the contents
of the crate began to float!

It was full of more than just steaks and fine roasts —
Up from the crate rose jam-covered toast!
There were biscuits of oats, brand new white coats,
brightly colored balls, and hooves of goats!
The crate contained so much more
than Charles's small dreaming,
so much more than his obsessing and scheming.

This treasure raced to the surface
with such vigor and force
that the two elder Pugsleys
were knocked off their course.

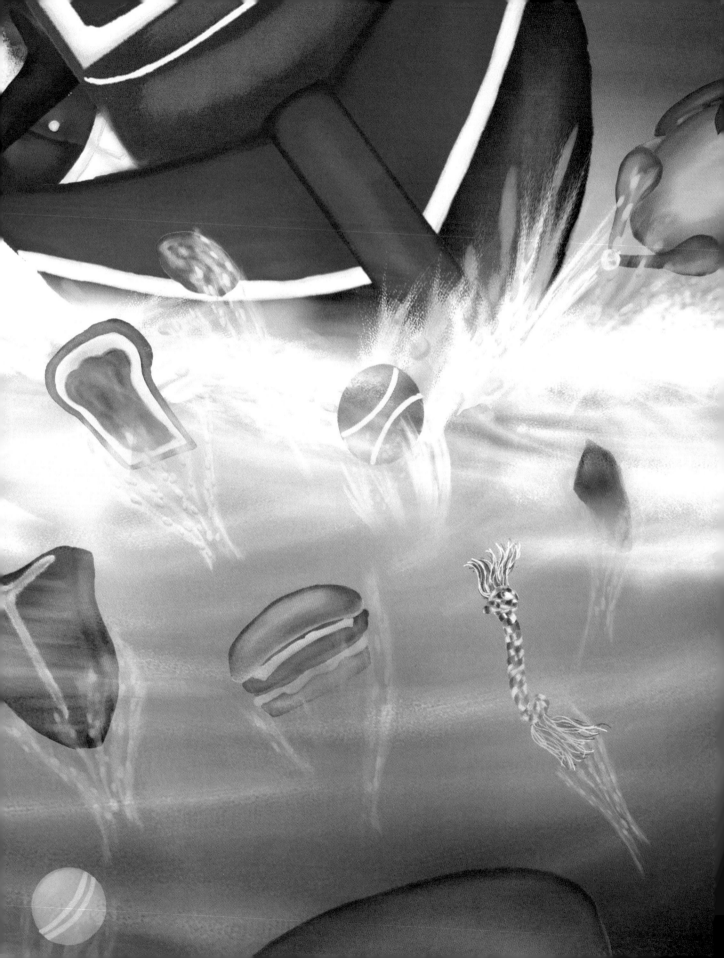

Father and Grandfather were flipped from their boat.
They landed in the water and were stripped of their small pug coats.
Settled next to Charles they saw it so clearly —
because of their haste and hurry they almost
lost the one they loved so dearly.
Here, too, they chose to let go of their worry.
And as the current carried them back to shore,
they knew they could not live as they had before.

Now the Pugsleys live as Grandfather had done so long ago.
They gather only for the day's needs — they never feel greedy,
they never feel poor, and they never feel needy.
When they are done with work for the day,
they head to the beach to play in the sand,
as treasures wash up daily
from the spilled crates onto the land.

In the sound of the waves that crash upon the shore,
a still, small voice calls out to each Charles,
a voice unlike the worried one before —
It whispers very quietly and it whispers with peace,
"Be at rest, your striving can cease.
Sometimes life *is* ruff, but do not worry,
there will always be enough."

The End.

Full Steam Ahead: A Pug Boat Family
1st Edition
ISBN: 9781079132236
Author: Laura Bergsma
Illustrations: Laura Bergsma
Book Design: Matthew Bergsma

See more of my work online
pantingportraits.com
Instagram: @laurabergsma.art

Acknowledgements
"Come to me, all you who are weary and burdened, and I will give you rest." — Matthew 11:28

Thanks to everyone who helped us finish this book
With a special thanks to @theotherhughjackman, for constantly nudging us along

More books by Laura Bergsma
See the "Backwards Blackbird" series, available on Amazon.com

More Charles Pugsley
Prints of "Pug Boat", more whimsical illustrations of dogs, and commissions
are available at pantingportraits.com

Made in the USA
Columbia, SC
29 July 2021